Baby Goose

KATE McMULLAN

PICTURES BY
PASCAL LEMAÎTRE

HYPERION BOOKS FOR CHILDREN
NEW YORK

TABLE OF CONTENTS

Old Mother Goose

Old Mother Goose, when she wants to wander,
Rides through the air on a very fine gander.
Wee baby geese behind her do fly,
Catching the wind as they sail through the sky.

Good Morning, Baby Goose

Donkey, Donkey, Soft and Gray

Donkey, donkey, soft and gray,
Open your mouth and gently bray;
Lift your ears and blow your horn,
To wake the babies this sleepy morn.

Pease Porridge Hot

Pease porridge hot, pease porridge cold, pease porridge in the pot, nine days old.

Some babies like it hot, some like it cold. Some like it in the pot, nine days old.

Oh, Baby Curly Locks

Oh, Baby Curly Locks,
Wilt thou be mine?
Thou shalt not wash dishes
Nor yet feed the swine,
But sit on a cushion
And sew a fine seam,
And feed upon strawberries,
Sugar, and cream.

Baby Griggs

Baby Griggs, Baby Griggs, she has seven different wigs.
She wears them up, she wears them down,
To please the people of the town.

1 MONDAY

2 TUESDAY

7 SUNDAY

3 WEDNESDAY

6 SATURDAY

5 FRIDAY

4 THURSDAY

She wears them east, she wears them west,
But she never can tell which she loves best.

Come, Butter, Come

Come, butter, come; come, butter, come;
Baby Kate stands at the gate,

Waiting for a butter cake.
Come, butter, come.

Pat-a-cake

Pat-a-cake, pat-a-cake,
  baker's man,
Bake me a cake
  as fast as you can;
Roll it and pat it
  and mark it with a B,
Put it in the oven
  for Baby and me.

Cock-a-doodle-do!

Cock-a-doodle-do!
Baby's lost his shoe!
Baby has looked everywhere
And knows not what to do!

Cock-a-doodle-do!
Baby's found his shoe!
Baby's put it on again,
Sing doodle-doodle-do!

9

Baby Shall Have a New Bonnet

Baby shall have a new bonnet,
And Baby shall go to the fair,
And Baby shall have a blue ribbon,
To tie up her bonnie brown hair.

Out and About, Baby Goose

Hark, Hark, the Dogs Do Bark

Hark, hark, the dogs do bark,
The babies are coming to town,
Some with flags, and some with bags,
And one in a velvet gown.

Seesaw, Baby

Seesaw, Baby, up and down,
Which is the way to Boston Town?
One foot up, the other foot down,
That is the way to Boston Town.

13

Oh, Baby Went a-Walking

Oh, Baby went a-walking and walked into a store;
He bought a pound of sausages and laid them on the floor.

Baby started singing La la la! a lively tune,
And all the little sausages danced around the room.

Dickery, Dickery Dare

Dickery, dickery dare,
The pig flew up in the air.
Run, Baby Brown!
Quick—bring him down!
Dickery, dickery dare.

Oh, the Baby Duke of York

Oh, the Baby Duke of York
He had ten thousand men,
He marched them up to the top of the hill,
And he marched them down again.

And when they were up,
   they were up,
And when they were down,
   they were down,
And when they were only halfway up,
They were neither up nor down.

Ride a Cockhorse

Ride a cockhorse to Banbury Cross, to see a fine baby upon a white horse;

Rings on her fingers and bells on her toes, she shall have music wherever she goes.

Splish-Splash, Baby Goose

Rain on the Green Grass

Rain on the green grass,
Rain on the tree,
Rain on the housetop,
But not on Baby.

Baby Foster Went to Gloucester

Baby Foster went to Gloucester

In a shower of rain.

He stepped in a puddle

Right up to his middle,

And never went there again.

Rub-a-dub Dub!

Rub-a-dub dub!
One, two, three in a tub,
With suds and bubbles for hair.
Baby Splasher, Baby Slosher,
Baby Soapy Face Washer—
Now off they go to the fair.

Big Mama Stood

Big Mama stood
   at the tub, tub, tub,
Three dirty babies
   she did rub, rub, rub;
But when they were clean,
And fit to be seen,
They all dressed up
   and danced on the green.

GREEN

23

This Is How Babies Take a Bath

This is how babies take a bath,
Take a bath, take a bath,
This is how babies take a bath,
On a cold and frosty morning!

Dance to your Daddy

Dance to your daddy, my little baby;

Dance to your daddy, my little lamb;

You shall have a fishy in a little dishy;

You shall have a fishy when the boat comes in.

Hark, Hark, the Dogs Do Bark

Hark, hark, the dogs do bark,
The babies are heading for home.
Some with hats, and some with cats,
And one with a brush and a comb.

Good Night, Baby Goose

The Man in the Moon

The man in the moon
Looked out of the moon,
Looked out of the moon and said,
"'Tis time for all the babies on the earth
To think about getting to bed."

There Was an Old Woman

There was an old woman
   who lived in a shoe,
She had so many babies,
   she knew not what to do.
She gave them some broth,
   she gave them some bread,
She sang them a song,
   and put them to bed.

Diddle, Diddle, Dumpling

Diddle, diddle, dumpling, Baby John,
Went to bed with his breeches on,
One sock off, and one sock on,
Diddle, diddle, dumpling, Baby John.

Rock-a-bye, Baby

Rock-a-bye, Baby, thy cradle is green,
Father's a nobleman, Mother's a queen,
Kitten's a lady and wears a gold ring,
Dog is a drummer and drums for the king.

Sleep, Baby, Sleep

Sleep, Baby, sleep,

Thy father guards the sheep;

Thy mother shakes the dreamland tree

And from it fall sweet dreams for thee,

Sleep, Baby, sleep.

Sleep, Baby, sleep,
Our cottage vale is deep;
The little lamb is on the green,
With woolly fleece so soft and clean—
Sleep, Baby, sleep.

33

Twinkle, Twinkle, Little Star

Twinkle, twinkle, little star,
Babies wonder what you are,
Up above the earth so high,
Like a diamond in the sky.

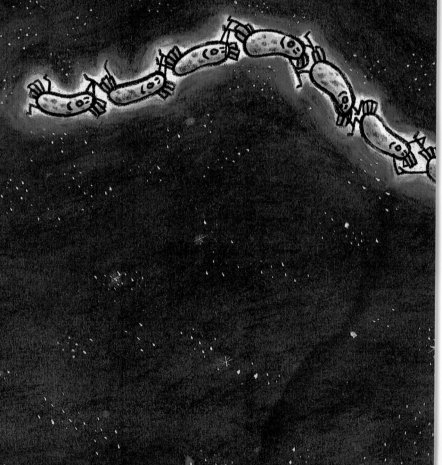

For Lily Grace Holland and her great-grandmother,
Grace Hall Kettenbrink
—K.M.

To my beloved baby, Maëlle,
and her mother, Manou, of course
—P.L.

Printed in Belgium
FIRST EDITION
1 3 5 7 9 10 8 6 4 2
Reinforced binding
Library of Congress Cataloging-in-Publication Data on file.
ISBN 0-7868-0430-0
Visit www.hyperionbooksforchildren.com